BEAUTY AND THE BEAST

A Favorite Story in Rhythm and Rhyme

Retold by JONATHAN PEALE

Illustrations by CHRISTINA LARKINS

Music by MARK OBLINGER

CANTATA
LEARNING

WWW.CANTATALEARNING.COM

CANTATA
LEARNING

Published by Cantata Learning
1710 Roe Crest Drive
North Mankato, MN 56003
www.cantatalearning.com

A note to educators and librarians from the publisher: Cantata Learning has provided the following data to assist in book processing and suggested use of Cantata Learning product.

Publisher's Cataloging-in-Publication Data
Prepared by Librarian Consultant: Ann-Marie Begnaud
Library of Congress Control Number: 2016938097
    Beauty and the Beast : A Favorite Story in Rhythm and Rhyme
    Series: Fairy Tale Tunes
    Retold by Jonathan Peale
    Illustrations by Christina Larkins
    Music by Mark Oblinger
    Summary: The classic fairy tale of Beauty and the Beast retold in song, with full-color illustrations.
    ISBN: 978-1-63290-767-7 (library binding/CD)
Suggested Dewey and Subject Headings:
    Dewey: E 398.2
    LCSH Subject Headings: Fairy tales – Juvenile literature. | Fairy tales – Songs and music – Texts. | Fairy tales – Juvenile sound recordings.
    Sears Subject Headings: Fairy tales. | School songbooks. | Children's songs.
    BISAC Subject Headings: JUVENILE FICTION / Fairy Tales & Folklore / Adaptations. | JUVENILE FICTION / Stories in Verse. | JUVENILE FICTION / Monsters.

Book design and art direction: Tim Palin Creative
Editorial direction: Flat Sole Studio
Music direction: Elizabeth Draper
Music written and produced by Mark Oblinger

Printed in the United States of America in North Mankato, Minnesota.
122016   0339CGS17

ACCESS THE MUSIC!

SCAN CODE WITH MOBILE APP

CANTATALEARNING.COM

TIPS TO SUPPORT LITERACY AT HOME

WHY READING AND SINGING WITH YOUR CHILD IS SO IMPORTANT

Daily reading with your child leads to increased academic achievement. Music and songs, specifically rhyming songs, are a fun and easy way to build early literacy and language development. Music skills correlate significantly with both phonological awareness and reading development. Singing helps build vocabulary and speech development. And reading and appreciating music together is a wonderful way to strengthen your relationship.

READ AND SING EVERY DAY!

TIPS FOR USING CANTATA LEARNING BOOKS AND SONGS DURING YOUR DAILY STORY TIME

1. As you sing and read, point out the different words on the page that rhyme. Suggest other words that rhyme.

2. Memorize simple rhymes such as Itsy Bitsy Spider and sing them together. This encourages comprehension skills and early literacy skills.

3. Use the questions in the back of each book to guide your singing and storytelling.

4. Read the included sheet music with your child while you listen to the song. How do the music notes correlate to the words of the song?

5. Sing along on the go and at home. Access music by scanning the QR code on each Cantata book, or by using the included CD. You can also stream or download the music for free to your computer, smartphone, or mobile device.

Devoting time to daily reading shows that you are available for your child. Together, you are building language, literacy, and listening skills.

Have fun reading and singing!

The fairy tale "Beauty and the Beast" was written in the 1700s. Like many fairy tales, it has a **moral**. Do you think you can figure out what lesson is hidden in this story?

To find out what it is, turn the page and sing along!

A **merchant** on a long, long trip
saw a garden, strange and fair,
and deep inside,
a perfect yellow rose was **blooming** there.

He thought of his gentle daughter, Beauty, and was sure she'd love that rose.

So he **plucked** the lovely flower. Then suddenly he froze!

7

A beast shouted, "You took my rose!
So I'll eat you for a treat!"

"Forgive me!" cried the merchant.
"It's for my daughter sweet!"

"Send me your daughter," growled the Beast.
"She'll live here with me!

And I'll spare your life!" So the merchant
hurried home, and Beauty, she agreed.

Beware. Beware.

Don't stir up the Beast!

You cannot run or hide!
If you stop and really look,
you may find
true beauty deep inside!

So Beauty lived with the horrible Beast,
and under her kind care,
the Beast grew tame and gentle
and learned to help and share.

But soon poor Beauty missed her home.
"I must return," she said.

The sad Beast said, "Then go,
and live with them instead."

Beware. Beware.

Don't stir up the Beast!

You cannot run or hide!
If you stop and really look,
you may find
true beauty deep inside!

Beauty returned to her father's house
and smiled, full of cheer!

Beast began to cry
because Beauty was not near.

Beauty heard that Beast was lonely
and hurried to his side.

"Poor Beast, I'm sorry I left.
I love you!" Beauty cried.

Then suddenly the ugly Beast
transformed into a prince.

"I was cursed by an evil witch
and was ugly ever since!

18

Only the love of another
could change my monster's **hide**!

Someone who truly cared
what I was like deep inside!"

Beware. Beware.
Don't stir up the Beast!

You cannot run or hide!
If you stop and really look,
you may find
true beauty deep inside!

Beware. Beware.
Don't stir up the Beast!

You cannot run or hide!
If you stop and really look,
you may find
true beauty deep inside!

SONG LYRICS
Beauty and the Beast

A merchant on a long, long trip
saw a garden, strange and fair,
and deep inside,
a perfect yellow rose was blooming there.

He thought of his gentle daughter,
    Beauty,
and was sure she'd love that rose.
So he plucked the lovely flower.
Then suddenly he froze!

A beast shouted, "You took my rose!
So I'll eat you for a treat!"
"Forgive me!" cried the merchant.
"It's for my daughter sweet!"

"Send me your daughter," growled
    the Beast.
"She'll live here with me!
And I'll spare your life!" So the merchant
hurried home, and, Beauty, she agreed!

Beware. Beware.
Don't stir up the Beast!
You cannot run or hide!
If you stop and really look,
you may find
true beauty deep inside!

So Beauty lived with the horrible Beast,
and under her kind care,
the Beast grew tame and gentle
and learned to help and share.

But soon poor Beauty missed her home.
"I must return," she said.
The sad Beast said, "Then go,
and live with them instead."

Beware. Beware.
Don't stir up the Beast!
You cannot run or hide!
If you stop and really look,
you may find
true beauty deep inside!

Beauty returned to her father's house
and smiled, full of cheer!
Beast began to cry
because Beauty was not near.

Beauty heard that Beast was lonely
and hurried to his side.
"Poor Beast, I'm sorry I left.
I love you!" Beauty cried.

Then suddenly the ugly Beast
transformed into a prince.
"I was cursed by an evil witch
and was ugly ever since!

Only the love of another
could change my monster's hide!
Someone who truly cared
what I was like deep inside!"

Beware. Beware.
Don't stir up the Beast!
You cannot run or hide!
If you stop and really look,
you may find
true beauty deep inside!

Beware. Beware.
Don't stir up the Beast!
You cannot run or hide!
If you stop and really look,
you may find
true beauty deep inside!

Beauty and the Beast

Musical Theater
Mark Oblinger

Verse

1. A mer - chant on a long, long trip saw a gar - den, strange and fair, and deep in - side, a per - fect yel - low rose was bloom - ing there. He thought of his gen - tle daugh - ter, Beau - ty, and was sure she'd love that rose. So he plucked the love - ly flow - er. Then sud - den - ly he froze!

Pre Chorus

A beast shout - ed, "You took my rose! So I'll eat you for a treat!" "For - give me!" cried the mer - chant. "It's for my daugh - ter sweet!" "Send me your daugh - ter," growled the Beast. "She'll live here with me!" "And I'll spare your life!" So the mer - chant hur - ried home, and, Beau - ty, she a - greed!

Chorus

Be - ware. Be - ware. Don't stir up the Beast! You can - not run or hide! If you stop and real - ly look, you may find true beau - ty deep in - side!

Verse 2
So Beauty lived with the horrible Beast,
and under her kind care,
the Beast grew tame and gentle
and learned to help and share.
But soon poor Beauty missed her home.
"I must return," she said.
The sad Beast said, "Then go,
and live with them instead."

Chorus

Verse 3

3. Beau - ty re - turned to her fa - ther's house and smiled, full of cheer! Beast be - gan to cry be - cause Beau - ty was not near. Beau - ty heard that Beast was lone - ly and hur - ried to his side. "Poor Beast, I'm sor - ry I left. I love you!" Beau - ty cried.

Pre chorus
Then suddenly the ugly Beast
transformed into a prince.
"I was cursed by an evil witch
and was ugly ever since!
Only the love of another
could change my monster's hide!
Someone who truly cared
what I was like deep inside!"

Chorus (x2)

GLOSSARY

beware—to look out for danger

blooming—to make flowers

hide—the skin of an animal

merchant—a person who buys and sells goods

moral—a lesson about what is right and wrong

plucked—to have picked something, such as a flower

transformed—changed from one form to another

GUIDED READING ACTIVITIES

1. The story of "Beauty and the Beast" teaches a moral, or a lesson. Can you think of any other stories that also have a moral? What lessons do they teach?

2. People wouldn't be friends with the Beast because of how he looked and acted. Do you think that was fair? Why or why not?

3. Beauty learns that the Beast is not who she thought he was at first. Has anything like this ever happened to you?

TO LEARN MORE

Meister, Cari. *Beauty and the Beast Stories around the World: Three Beloved Tales*. North Mankato, MN: Capstone, 2017.

Moses, Will. *Fairy Tales for Little Folks*. New York: Viking, 2015.

Roumanis, Alexis. *Beauty and the Beast*. New York: AV2 by Weigl, 2016.

Steig, Jeanne. *A Handful of Beans: Six Fairy Tales*. New York: Atheneum Books for Young Readers, 2016.